In memory of the Columbia 7

Atheneum Books for Young Readers

An imprint of Simon & Schuster Children's Publishing Division

1230 Avenue of the Americas, New York, New York 10020

Book design by Ann Bobco

The text for this book is set in Granjon.

The illustrations for this book are rendered in watercolor, colored pencils, and litho pencils.

Manufactured in China

First Edition

2 4 6 8 10 9 7 5 3 1

Library of Congress Cataloging-in-Publication Data

Colón, Raúl.

Orson blasts off! / Raúl Colón.— 1st ed.

p. cm.

"An Anne Schwartz Book."

Summary: When his computer breaks down, a little boy discovers that imagination is way more fun than a computer game.

ISBN 0-689-84278-3

[1. Imagination—Fiction. 2. Play—Fiction.] I. Title.

PZ7.C716365Or 2004

[E]—dc21

2003045362

JE
Colón
May 14, 2004

RAÚL COLÓN

ORSON BLASTS OFF!

An Anne Schwartz Book • Atheneum Books for Young Readers

New York   London   Toronto   Sydney   Singapore

"Oh, no!!!"

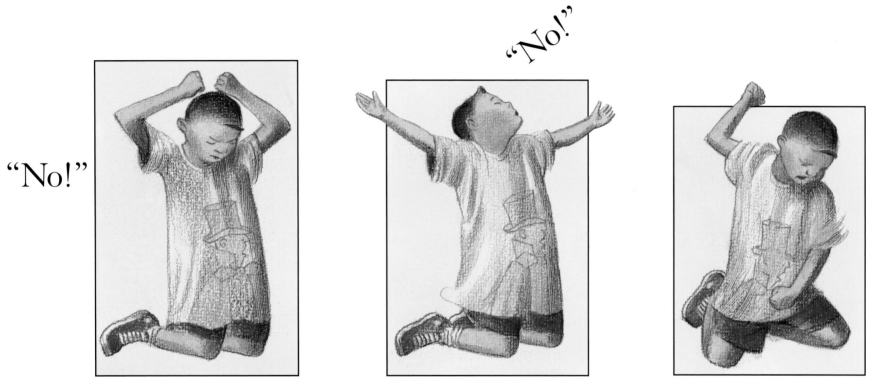

"No!" "No!" "No!"

"You dumb computer, how could you? Now there's no way I can play
Arctic Adventure, or Whale Storm, or Starship Boomerang, or anything.

"Rats! I think I'm bored already!"

Tick Tock. Tick Tock. Tick Tock.

"Ahem! Orson? Excuse me, sir. No need to get upset."

"Who's that?"

"It is I, Weasel.
May I kindly ask you to step outside?"

"Outside? I don't *do* outside. Anyway, all that's there is a bunch of snow. Hey, wait a minute—snow? In July? And . . . you can talk?"

"There certainly is, sir. And I certainly can."

"Yahoo, snow in July! Now, let's see. I'll need my jacket and gloves, these old tennis rackets, some bungee cords, my backpack, and . . ."

"Orson, sir, I kindly beg you to need *me*."

"Okay, okay. . . . And I'll need you, too, Weasel.

"And that must be a southerly breeze—or are you breathing down my neck?"

"Respectfully, sir, it is not I, and it is not a breeze . . . unless a breeze is white and round with big, dark eyes and giant paws."

"Sir, I think we're trapped. The water looks remarkably chilly, and I believe I see a storm approaching."

"Don't worry, Weasel. I have an idea that should get us out of here."

"You'd better fold fast, sir."

"You know, some storms have eyes, Weasel. And if this one does, and it can see us, maybe it won't hurt us."

"Maybe, sir. Why, there's an eye!"

"Y-e-e-e-s-s-s-s! We're saved."

"Captain Orson, the boat is about to sink. I suggest you hold on to your hat."

"Wow! Wait till I tell my buddies about this, Weasel. It'll sure make one whale of a tale."

"Or, if you'll pardon me, sir, one tail of a whale!"

"Am I glad to be back on dry land!
Just look at those stars, Weasel."

"They're twinkling at us, sir."

"Which gives me another idea . . ."

"Sir, please. You can't possibly think your idea will fly."

"Of course it will. Give me a hand and start the countdown."

"Ten . . . *this is madness* . . . seven, six, five . . . *madness, I say* . . . two, one . . ."

"Just look at those stars and those planets and those comets and those meteors and those moons! Isn't that the Big Dipper? I love it!"

"I'm glad someone does, sir."

"I think I see a black hole ahead.
Let's get closer."

"Why would we want to do that, sir?"

"Why *wouldn't* we want to?"

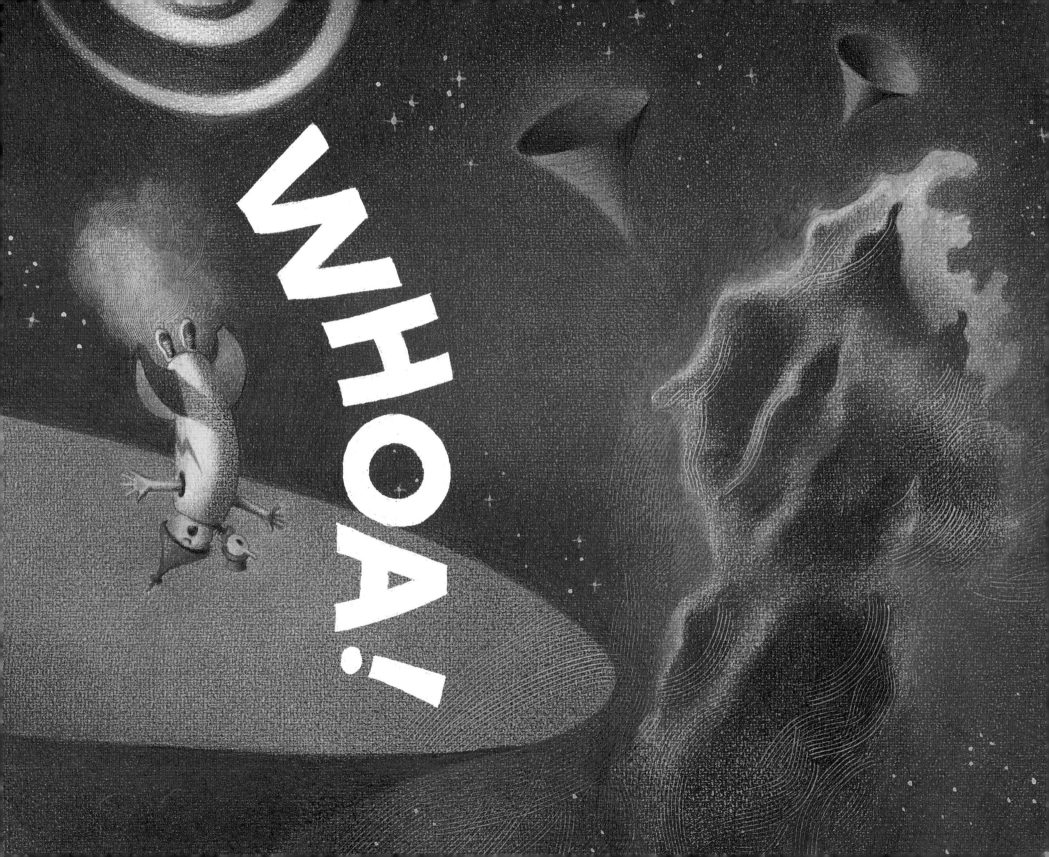

"Orson, sir, it appears
we're falling!
Falling down!
Falling up!
Falling sideways!"

TICK TOCK. TICK TOCK. TICK TOCK.

"Hey, Weasel, we're home. That was some trip, wasn't it, little guy?

Hey, Weasel, are you asleep? Oh well, I guess I'll go play . . .

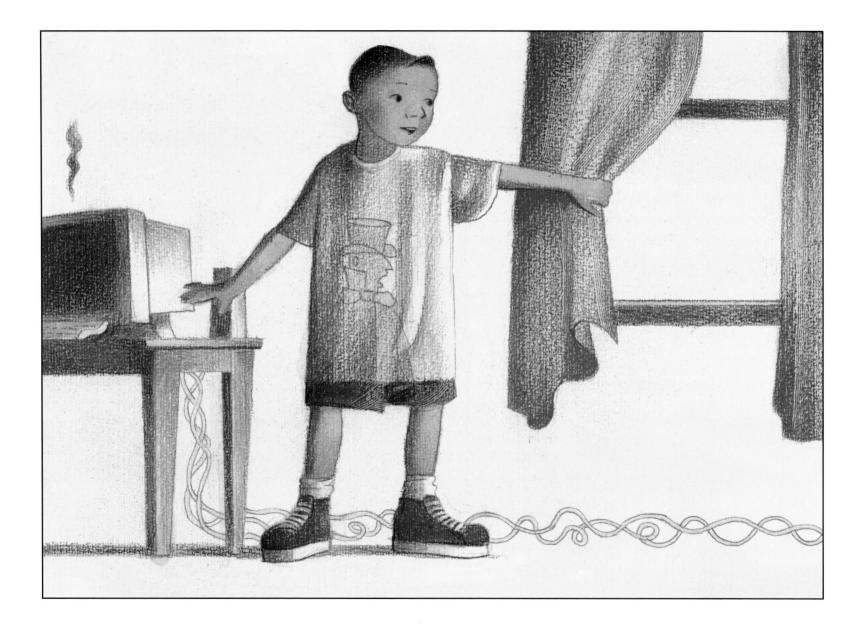

". . . outside."

A Note About the Text

Orson Blasts Off! plays with scientific terms and idiomatic expressions—phrases that do not mean what they appear to mean. They are, in order of appearance:

North Pole: This is not a pole in the ground, but the final destination for travelers who follow their compass needle north from anywhere on Earth.

eye of the storm: At the center of a cyclone or hurricane, all is calm, as winds, rain, and thunder rage around it. There is little or no cloud cover here. This is called the "eye" of the storm, although there is no real eye.

hold on to your hat: This is an expression that means "prepare yourself for a wild ride." You don't literally need to be wearing a hat for someone to say this to you.

whale of a tale: This phrase—not necessarily about our largest mammal—can mean any very exaggerated or impressive story.

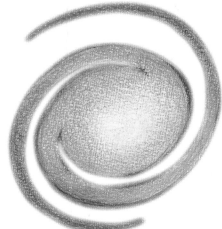

[an] idea [that] will fly: This expression comes from a time when many harebrained (another idiomatic expression!) contraptions were built to fly . . . and often didn't. An idea flies—just like a flying machine—when it *works*.

Big Dipper: Part of the constellation Ursa Major, it was given its name because its seven bright stars form the shape of a bowl and handle.

black hole: This is an astronomical term referring to a region of space where mass is so great that nothing—not even light—can escape its gravitational pull.

JE   Colon, Raul.

Orson blasts off!